The Purple Girl

a story by

Audrey Kane

Illustrations by Tory & Norman Taber

Wakefield & Quincy Press

The Purple Girl

This book is a work of fiction. Names, characters, places and incidents are the products of the author's imagination or are used fictitiously. Any resemblance to actual events, locales, or persons, living or dead, is entirely coincidental.

First Edition, January 2014

Illustrations by Tory & Norman Taber
www.toryandnormantaber.com

Book Layout and Formatting by Pedernales Publishing, LLC.
www.pedernalespublishing.com

Published by Wakefield & Quincy Press

Library of Congress Control Number: 2014930320

ISBN: 978-0-9910283-1-3 Paperback
ISBN: 978-0-9910283-2-0 e-Book
ISBN: 978-0-9910283-3-7 Audio

Printed in the United States of America

To order additional copies of this title, contact a local bookstore or visit *www.audreykane.com*

With special thanks to: Heidi Giusto, Ph.D,
Tory and Norman Taber, Ramona Long, Christopher
Laney, Jose Ramirez, and Barbara Rainess.

For Andrew
Lauren, Ryan, and Caroline
—my whole heart

We are what we believe we are.

C. S. Lewis

The Purple Girl

England of Long Ago…

Chapter One

THE BABY

This is how the story was told to me.

When the midwife brought me into the world, she let out a scream. Hands trembling, she swaddled me in a white blanket, leaving only a small opening so I could breathe. She refused to let my mother see me until my father appeared and stood by her side. Purple mist seeped through the white blanket, staining the midwife's fingers.

"God help us all. This baby is cursed!" the midwife cried, thrusting me into my father's arms. She grabbed a rag and tried to scrub the stains off her hands.

As my father unwrapped me, the color drained from his face. My mother, weak from the delivery, reached toward him...or perhaps to me.

"What's wrong?"

After a moment, he held me up.

My mother wailed when she saw her purple baby.

My father turned away from her and laid me in the cradle, far from my mother, his fingers shaking as he bundled me in the plum-colored blanket. He remained silent, wiping his purple stained palms on his pants. The stains wouldn't stay on him forever… only a few moments…but he didn't know that then.

"Oh, Samuel," my mother sobbed. "How did this happen?"

My father gazed into my eyes, and when he finally spoke, his voice broke.

"We'll call her Violet." He stroked a tuft of my lavender hair and sank to his knees.

The midwife eyed my father before she whispered. "I can take her into the forest and bury her there, as if she never—"

My father sprang to his feet, his eyes blazing with anger.

The woman took a step back, then snatched her leather satchel and bolted through the door. My parents never saw the midwife again.

Chapter Two

THE OUTCAST

It was late in the evening, and flickering candlelight spilled from underneath the door of our cottage's front room. When I cracked open the door, I found my father sitting at his desk with his head bent over an open book. A small fire crackled in the fireplace.

I slipped into the room.

With his head still in the book, Papa furrowed his brow.

I crept up beside him and peeked over his shoulder.

Papa jerked upright. "You startled me," he said, nudging me away. His spectacles slipped down the bridge of his nose. His face was long like mine, his forehead high. His snowy white hair made him appear older than his years.

I spotted a velvet book-cover lying on the desk. Tiny silver bells dangled along the edges. I eyed the book again. "What are you reading?"

Papa snapped the book shut.

I tilted my head sideways, trying to steal a glance.

He pulled the book close to his chest but not before I caught a glimpse of it. "It's covered in *jewels*!"

"This book doesn't concern you, Violet."

"All the more tempting! *Please* let me look at it."

"Absolutely not. Your purple spreads to whatever you touch..."

"...and fades away once I'm not touching it," I finished.

"This is different." As he slipped the book back into its velvet cover, it jingled. "It's old—the pages are delicate, and the cover is fragile." He took off his spectacles and laid them on the desk. "And it's late," he said, rubbing his tired eyes.

"You're treating me like a child."

"This isn't an ordinary book, Violet."

"Ordinary books don't have rubies and—"

"And you're *thirteen*. A man has to be thirty

years of age or older before reading it," he said, frowning. "And even at that age...you will be a *woman*. It's forbidden for you to even touch it." He pushed his chair away from the desk and got to his feet. "You should be in bed by now."

"But how did you get a book—*covered in jewels*?"

He turned to the bookshelf and slipped it back into place.

"And where—"

"Enough questions for one night, Violet."

"Answer at least one. Please, Papa."

He turned to me and sighed, his voice wavering when he finally replied. "My father gave it to me, and his father gave it to him. It is passed from father to son."

"But you don't have a son," I whispered.

"Upstairs, Violet, to bed," he said, raising his voice. "Now."

I WOKE EARLY the next morning. Before I went out into the garden, I tucked up my long skirt into my waistband so I could move easily among the rows of vegetables. I managed this way, alone, singing...

protected by our cottage and the walled gardens surrounding it, the walls my father built after my birth. My little dog, Waxy, nosed my ankles.

Mama popped her head out of the window. "We're going into the village."

I stood stock-still. "*I'm* going?"

Mama nodded. "It's time to try again."

It was a moment or two before I took in the meaning. I brushed the lavender dirt off my skirt and darted into the cottage. Waxy trotted behind me.

Perched on my chair, I leaned toward the mirror and frowned. It was all there. Lavender eyes, purple curls, brows too violet, and cheeks too plum. *No escaping.* When I pulled on my coffee-colored dress, shades of violet suddenly surfaced from the brown weave and spilled through the buttons. I threw my hands up in frustration and let out a scream.

Mama appeared in the doorway. "Violet, we've been through this before."

When I didn't answer, Mama touched my shoulder. "Here," she said, handing me a black cloak.

Spinning away from the mirror, I slipped on the cloak and pulled the hood over my head. Shades of lavender rippled through it, then deepened into plum. I shot my mother a look.

"It can't hide you—but at least you're not in plain sight," she said, placing her hands on her knobby hips. "Hurry, please. We're out of flour." She led me out the door and past my father.

"Be *careful*," he warned.

"How much trouble could I get into—a girl like me?" I asked, glancing back at him with a weak smile, hoping the tremble in my voice didn't betray me.

As my parents exchanged a look, my mother patted the small cloth satchel at her side. "I have the knife," she whispered.

We walked toward the bakery on a dirt road lined with twisted oaks. "Girls my age can walk by themselves," I said, dodging a pothole.

"You aren't like girls your age," my mother countered. A loose strand of her mousy brown hair fell from her bun.

"Have you ever peeked in Papa's book? You know the one—"

"What book?"

I considered telling Mama about the forbidden text, but I liked having a secret. "Oh, just a book. Nothing special."

As voices rose from a nearby cottage, a maid poked her head out of a window. When she caught sight of me, she slammed it shut. The window locks clicked.

Mama lifted her pointy chin and quickened her step. "We are almost to the bakery," she said, taking my hand. My purple crept up hers and then trickled up her wrist.

I pulled my hand away. "Aren't you a little old to hold hands, Mama?" I asked with a smile.

We passed Widow Collin's cottage and Wakefield Place and Dragonfly Hill, where thatched cottages stood closer to one another, edging the road. With the exception of green leaves brushing blue sky, the bleak town was washed in tones of dirty pail water—but it looked exciting to me.

"Two more twists on the road before we reach the bakery." Mama's voice wavered. "I'm proud of you, Violet, for being brave enough to try again." We made our way down the road and past a cobbler who was setting up a stall at the outdoor market. "It's hard being the...*only* one," she whispered.

We walked by the cathedral, built in grander times, and then toward the bell-tower where a larger-than-life statue of an angel stood guard by the entrance. Her granite arms seemed to reach out to me.

My eyes dropped to her feet. Someone had painted her toenails blue! *Who is the prankster? And where did he get blue paint?* Biting back my smile, I slowed my step and peered past her, craning my neck toward the bell-tower that loomed overhead.

"Move along, Violet. We haven't much time. They'll be busy soon. The bakery will be full of people."

I broke out in goose-bumps, understanding what she meant. *People.* My heart raced as she led me up the walk and to the crumbling front door.

Mama hesitated and then glanced back at me.

I drew a deep breath before stepping forward. *Must not be afraid.*

Chapter Three

THE OFFER

The fragrance of warm bread laced the hot spongy air as Mama exchanged pleasantries with the baker's wife. The baker's daughter, a girl blessed with pale skin and an average face, kneaded a ball of dough on the long table.

I caught my reflection in the window and then gazed down at my purple hands, wishing they were milky white. Or nut-brown. Or any other—

"The devil's child is back," said the daughter, nodding at me. She twisted her rosebud lips into a sneer.

A coldness shot through me.

My mother stiffened before she gave me an unexpected peck on the cheek.

"Mama!" I felt my face flush.

Mama took the bag of flour and laid a few coins on the table. My violet was already fading from her lips.

The baker's wife scooped up the coins.

The girl stopped kneading. She folded her flour-dusted arms and narrowed her dark eyes at me. "Look at what you've done already," she said, pointing to the purple stained floor underneath my feet. "You're *lucky* we sell to you."

"But—"

"How dare you parade around in the daylight, where people have to see—"

"This is the first time she's left their cottage in five months," said the baker's wife.

"And three days," I added. "Not since—"

"Thank you for the flour," Mama snapped, her face hardening. "And good day," she called to the baker's wife as she opened the door.

I felt a catch in my throat and swallowed hard.

"Hold your head high," mother whispered just loud enough for me to hear. Drawing her satchel close to her, she pinched her lips and stared straight ahead as I followed her down the walk. "The superstitious girl, why she can't read her own name. But *you* can read a book." She sighed, adding quietly, "You are a most unusual girl, Violet."

"There are other things I would rather be."

"I shouldn't have encouraged you to come. The villagers are suffering, and children are sent to workhouses." She paused to wipe her brow. "In some ways, you are lucky."

"Lucky? That's the second time I've heard that one today." Through the willow hedge, I caught sight of Holy, the farmer's cow. Holy Cow stood alone in the pasture.

I looked at my mother. "Do you want to know what I think, Mama? I'll tell you what I think. If I knew *why*—"

"If I knew, I would tell you. Besides, it doesn't matter."

"It matters to me," I replied, struggling to keep up with my mother's long legs. I glanced back at the vanishing violet trail my footsteps left.

We climbed two jagged stone steps and then stopped outside the shop. "Wait out here. If the butcher sees you—"

"I know, Mama. I remember." I shivered, pushing the painful recollection away. *We have the satchel now, the one with the knife.*

She hesitated, biting on her bottom lip. "It may take a few minutes," she said, handing me the bag of flour. We turned our heads toward the rumbling of a wagon. As the horse and buggy plodded by, I melted into the shadows.

"Violet—"

"I'm not afraid, Mama. Go on." I held the bag of flour with one hand and nudged her forward with the other.

"Take care with the flour." She glanced around once more before disappearing behind the door.

I was accustomed to solitude, but the more time I spent alone, the more I longed for others. So, I filled the silence like I usually did—singing. I sang quieter than a whispering wind, hummed softer than falling snow.

An errand boy rushed by, carrying a parcel under each arm, the sun kissing his honey-blond hair. Afraid of being seen, I turned my back to him and gazed the other way—where I spotted her. *A gypsy girl! Just like the picture in my book...*

The gypsy looked about my age, maybe a little older. Her long, straight hair was pulled back from her face, and large hoop rings dangled from her earlobes. When she spotted me, she stopped short.

She mumbled to herself and waved her bony, ring-covered fingers through the air in a circular motion. With her other hand curled around a tin cup, she started forward, inching her way closer to me.

I stopped humming.

"Would you like a reading?" she asked, brushing my hand with her fingertip.

I stepped back, surprised. *She touched me!* "A reading?" I stammered, meeting her large brown eyes. Her fingertips picked up my purple tint, but she didn't seem to notice.

"Your fortune, silly girl. A sixpence," she said, her scratchy voice splitting.

"I don't have a sixpence," I answered, eyeing her with care.

"Miss Peculiar doesn't have a sixpence?" she cackled, tilting her head.

A chill skipped down my spine, yet I couldn't pull my eyes away. "My name is Violet."

"You even *smell* like a violet. What's in your purple bag, *Violet*?"

"Flour."

"Hmmm. Give me your palm," she said, grabbing my hand. She turned it over and traced the lines of my open palm. My purple crept up her hand, but instead of jerking away, she traced more lines. "I'll read your future, a girl like you."

"What do you mean, a girl like me?" The words spilled out of my mouth. "What about you? You're a *gypsy* girl. There aren't—"

"You have a golden key!"

"A what?"

"You're hiding it," she said mysteriously, still studying my palm.

"But I don't have a key."

"It's like a…winning ticket. But it's the key." Her eyes widened, and her mouth dropped open.

"What?"

She started to speak but changed her mind.

"Tell me!"

"You will never throw the bridal bouquet."

I yanked my hand away. "Never get married?" Why this obvious conclusion surprised or upset me, I'll never know, but my eyes filled with tears.

"Every young maiden wants a lad. Even you." Her strangled voice had a painful edge to it, almost a shrill. "You're not *so* different. My grandmother…" she shifted her eyes left to right, "can cast a spell, one that will change *everything*." The gypsy girl grinned and dipped her empty cup into my flour.

"What do you mean?" I closed the bag, clutching it close to me.

"She can make your purple disappear." Her brown eyes locked with my violet ones as she leaned toward me and whispered, "But you have to give me something."

My guard went up. "What do you want?"

"Hmmm..." She drummed her fingers against her thigh. "You have curl to your hair," she cooed, reaching out to me, winding one of my purple curls around her forefinger. "As if your purple hood could hide them," she said, letting the curl slip free. "But your gift has to be as precious as mine. You have a...mother?"

"Mama?" I gasped, choking on the thought.

"I'm not asking for your mother," she reassured me with a wicked grin. "I'm simply asking: What do you have? My grandmother will be sprinkling the last of the holy herbs on *you*, Violet."

When an image of Waxy crossed my mind, I pushed it aside. "We have a garden."

"Gypsies trek the world. I can't take a garden with me, but you know that. You're a *clever* purple girl," she taunted, her bracelets clinking against one another. "But if you don't have anything, and you like the way things are—"

"My father has a rare book, but I don't—"

"I've had plenty of offers for books. Books weigh you down. They just remind us of what we already know in here," she said, tapping her heart. "And what gypsy reads? Unless your book is one of the missing texts—one with all the answers?" She lifted a dark eyebrow and leaned back laughing. "Of course not! If you knew all the answers, you wouldn't be talking to me—would you, *Violet*?"

I felt confused. "How about the quilt Mama stitched for me?"

"You're trying to take something without sacrificing...*anything*." She tilted her head and searched my purple face. "But it's your intellect I like. I would take your sense of humor, but you don't have much of one."

Her voice sounded rusty and harsh. Hearing it made me want to swallow, as if the scratchiness was catching. I wiped my damp palms against my legs.

"It has to be something I can carry with me," she said, tapping her chin. "I know. How about your golden key?"

"But I told you, I don't have a golden key."

"If not your golden key...or your mother, how about...your voice box?"

I felt my mouth drop open.

"You have a *purr* to your voice," she told me, shrugging her shoulders.

"Your grandmother's spell...will make my purple go away?" My throat started to itch.

"Would I lie to *you*, Violet? You'll throw the bridal bouquet and have children...but your children will not be born," she poked at my purple skin, "to *suffer*. You could go anywhere, be *anyone*. If you give me your voice box, a new—"

"My voice box," I repeated, touching the base of my throat.

"It's a small price to pay, don't you think?" She grinned as her voice scratched on. "One change, changes *everything*."

Mama's voice chimed through the door.

"Meet me here, tomorrow, at dawn, before my family leaves for the mountains," the gypsy spouted, eyeing the door. "I'll take you to a hidden place—"

I heard Mama's footsteps and gazed toward the door.

"Will I get your voice? Or will I be a girl *without* a voice?" I pictured myself gagging and choking up chunks of silent words.

"My grandmother will agree to do this, for *me*, and I am willing to—"

The knob on the door turned. My mother appeared. "Violet?"

I turned to the gypsy girl, but she was gone.

THAT NIGHT I got into my bed and nestled underneath my quilt. Watching the full moon inch by, I lay there wide awake thinking about the gypsy's offer. But it would cost me.

And Papa? *A forbidden book. Secrets! Well, I have secrets, too...*

My throat began to itch as I drifted in and out of a troubled sleep. When I finally opened my eyes again, the answer came to me. I climbed out of bed and dressed before I tiptoed down the dark staircase.

Chapter Four

THE ANCIENT TEXT

The wood creaked beneath me as I crept down the stairs and found my way to the front room where the embers in the fireplace still burned.

I took a candle stub from the mantel and lit the wick with the embers. In the soft glow of the orange candlelight, I lingered by the bookshelves and ran my fingers against the spines, searching for the ancient volume, reading title after title until my finger stopped on the velvet cover. *If Papa kept this on the bookshelf, why haven't I have noticed it before?* I stood the candle bit in a holder and then pulled out the *Text of Wisdom*. As I slipped off the velvet book-cover, it jingled.

I froze.

To my relief, the soft and steady snores of my parents reached my ears. I let out my breath slowly and peered at the jewel-encrusted book, tracing one of the blue jewels with my fingertip until it glistened with lavender light. I felt a smile spread across my face.

I laid the book on my father's desk and opened it. On the inside cover, someone had written a long list of names and birthdates in silver ink. I paused when I saw the last name scrawled at the bottom of the page: *Violet.*

In the flickering candlelight, I combed through the index and then flipped through the pages until my eyes finally landed upon it.

Golden Key:

1. *An ancient term that identifies descendents of the original royal bloodline.*

2. *A mystical key that unlocks one's very soul.*

A scribbled note in the margin read:

Each golden key is uniquely cut to fit a specific mortal.

In the unsteady light, I lingered over the book until my purple blotches faded from the page. Suddenly, a new thought darted through my mind. I raked through the book's index before I found it.

Larynx:

1. *The hollow organ that holds the vocal chords; often referred to as the Voice Box.*

2. *Considered holy by some, ancient legends WARN—*

To my dismay, dark stains smeared the rest of the sentence. I picked up the candle and held it closer, struggling to decipher the words, but the letters were smudged.

I flipped back to the index, searching for the words *purple or skin or violet-colored.*

Nothing.

Frustrated, I blew out the candle and slipped the book back into its velvet cover.

"Violet, is that you?" my mother called from her bed.

I gave a little gasp. With the text in my hands and my heart pounding, I stood rooted to the spot. There was a second of silence, and then I heard the creak of her bed and the easy rhythm of her snores.

Barely breathing, I replaced the text on the shelf and then crept my way through the doorway toward the kitchen. There wasn't much time. Dawn was ready to break. The gypsy girl would be waiting.

When I reached the side door, I hesitated. *Can I do this?* The garden is a pretty but also a lonely place to be caged in.

With unsteady hands, I eased open the door and slipped out.

Chapter Five

EAVESDROPPER

I scooted down our footpath and sprinted into the pre-dawn light. My heart hammered, and except for the rhythm of my breath, the world remained silent. The town slept as I ran past.

I had never felt so free. Even my purple dimmed in the early light, or so I thought. Finally out of breath, I slowed to a steady walk. The fragrance of dry leaves and rosemary laced the air, and a bird chirped, welcoming a pink tip of sun. Ahead of me, I caught sight of the gypsy girl hiding in the morning shadows.

"Come on," she said, waving me forward. "We don't have much time."

I felt uneasy. "But, what—"

"Follow me," She turned her steps toward the forest and rushed down an embankment. I followed close behind as she weaved her way through the twisted trees and across a creek. When she glanced back at me, her crooked smile widened with mischief.

I hurried, trailing behind her as she threaded her way through the forest and then disappeared behind overgrown shrubs. I followed her, skirting around a tangle of bramble, leaping over fallen limbs. Twigs snapped. Leaves rustled. We ducked under branches and pushed our way through the mazelike forest until we reached a meadow dusted with coral wildflowers.

Without a backward glance, the waif-like gypsy girl darted across the meadow, her black skirt billowing in the wind. And although I ran as fast as my legs could carry me, I lagged behind until she suddenly slowed.

When I finally caught up with her, I tried to catch my breath, but she took off again. We ran until we reached an odd branch of the forest where the grass thinned and jagged boulders towered overhead, touching the wide blue sky.

"Over here," she gestured, waving her arm

toward a crowd of boulders. She darted along the basin of one of the rocks and then stopped to glance back at me, as if making sure I was still behind her. When our eyes met, I was sure we shared a sense of excitement, and for a fleeting moment, I forgot I was purple.

The gypsy girl turned back to the rock wall. Sweeping aside a veil of hanging vines, she stepped toward the boulder and vanished.

I followed her path along the base of the rock until I reached the hanging vines. When I pushed them aside, I saw a crevice that was just wide enough for me to slip through. My heart thumped against my ribcage. Did I dare?

I took a deep breath and plunged into the drafty darkness, feeling my way along the cold edge of the rock. Seconds later, I emerged on the other side.

Light blinded me. As my eyes adjusted, I heard the sound of padded steps behind me.

"Waxy! What are you doing here?" I squealed.

"Over here," the gypsy girl said. She ushered me up a path until we came to two natural springs. The first pool glimmered with turquoise water but puffed out red steam. A foul odor hung in the air, moldy and sour and heavy with rot. I held my breath and turned to the second pool, which bubbled and gurgled and spit out chunks of pasty, white mud.

Padded steps rushed from behind, and golden fur swished in front of me while little, white paws climbed my legs.

"Waxy! Go home," I ordered, pushing him away from the gurgling lava. *Could* he find his way back home? Heat rose from the earth and through the thin soles of my shoes, slowly cooking my feet.

"Come on," she said, edging closer to the bubbling pool of mud.

"Move, Waxy." The little guy whined, then danced on my warm feet as I tried to nudge him out of the way.

"We don't have much time!" the gypsy girl shrilled, waving me toward her. "Come on, Violet."

"Go home, Waxy!"

"Don't you want to change your fate?"

"Go!" I cried, afraid he wouldn't. My feet began to burn. I stood on one foot, then shifted to the other.

"Don't you want to throw the bridal bouquet?"

Waxy turned toward the gypsy girl and let out a growl.

"Come with me, but leave the viper," she screeched, stepping back. "Or…we could give him a bath, one he'll *never* forget." She glanced at the bubbling lava. "What do you say, Purple Girl?"

Her words stopped me cold.

"My grandmother needs a dog's paw for a spell—"

"Come on, Waxy!" Fury filled my eyes while terror filled the rest of me. Letting my fading lavender footsteps lead the way, I sprinted back toward the bolder.

"Come back! Please!"

I glanced over my shoulder as Waxy charged in front of me.

"You have the golden k-e-e-e-y," the girl howled, dropping to her knees. "You'll be *sor-r-ry*!"

I slipped back into the rock's crevice and inched my way along the rock's jagged wall until I reached the opposite side. Stopping only to catch my breath, I dashed along the base of the rock basin. Waxy led me across the creek and the meadow, through the tangled forest, and up the embankment until we found ourselves back on the road, exhausted and relieved, headed for home.

THE NEXT MORNING dawned bright. *What are Mama and Papa whispering about in the front room?* I stood by the open doorway listening.

"The drought caused more crops to fail. The villagers are rioting and blaming each other for bad luck. Some blame Violet. Shattered glass—"

Papa whispered something I couldn't catch.

My mother gasped. "I had trouble buying flour. And not because of Violet," she murmured.

"The mill is letting me stay on," Papa replied, reassuring her in his low, steady voice.

"We've been through worse." A moment of unspoken understanding rippled between them. "Much worse."

I knew he meant me.

"Did you know the villagers are stealing food?" Mama asked, dropping her voice. "I don't know how long our garden will be safe. They've always been too afraid to come here, but…"

I melted farther into the shadows, straining to hear more, my ear pressed to the wall.

"The ceiling collapsed in the schoolhouse, the bells in the bell-tower are broken, the people are desperate, there is blood on the cobblestones—"

I hiccupped.

"Violet?" Papa got to his feet.

"I heard you say something about the bell-tower," I stammered, stepping out of the shadows. Mama remained seated on her chair. Above her hung the one picture we owned: a simple drawing in blue pencil of a mother holding her child. A miniature statue of a rabbit rested on a weathered table. "The bells need to be fixed."

"There isn't money to tend to the bells," Mama told me. "Nor time to fix them."

"But the bells are the heart of the village," I said.

Papa reached out to me and stroked my cheek. "The tomatoes, remember?"

"Already threw out the rotten ones," I said, hiccupping again before I made my way to the garden. Trying to quiet my tangled thoughts, I dropped five good tomatoes into my basket and rang out one smooth creamy song after another. I sang to myself, sang to Waxy, sang to our silent garden. When the rustle of a tree caught my attention, my singing came to a halt.

I turned my head toward the stone fence and crept toward it.

"Over here," a voice called to me.

I followed along the wall my father built. It rose about three feet above my head.

"I'm over here."

By the far end of the garden, a small hole pierced the wall where a few rocks had given way. I peeped through. A blue eye stared back.

"Thought I heard someone," the voice said.

My face flushed.

"Stay there. I'm climbing over."

A pair of dirty hands appeared on top of the wall. Seconds later, a boy with honey-blond hair and a square jaw emerged as he pulled himself up and onto the wall. There he sat, with his long, muscular legs dangling over the rough stone.

He took a good look at me before he pushed himself off the wall and into my garden.

Chapter Six

THE LOOK-OUT GIRL

The boy landed in my garden. "Aren't you afraid of me?"

"Why would I be afraid of you?" He brushed his sooty hands on his tattered knickers. "You're just a—girl." Although his shoulders were broad, his clothes hung limply on his lean body.

"You're not afraid of my purple?"

"I find it..." he paused, "refreshing."

I suppressed a smile. I had been called many things before but never *refreshing*!

Soot was smeared across one of his cheeks, and his tan skin glistened with sweat. He gave a sideways glance before he sprinted toward a corner of the garden wall. "How many friends have you invited into your garden?" he asked, dangling a mouse by the end of its pink-tipped tail.

I gasped.

Flashing a crooked smile, the boy lunged toward me with the mouse. I turned and darted around a huckleberry bush.

"Not a rodent lover, Purple Girl? Anything else I should know?"

He was only two purple steps behind! I shrieked.

A window creaked open. "Violet?" Mama called from the cottage.

The boy released the mouse and stood in the shadows.

"Just mouse…ing around," I hollered, trying to catch my breath.

The boy shot me a smile.

When the window snapped shut, I dropped into the grass.

The boy plunked down beside me. "You're fast, for a girl."

"That's only one of my many attributes," I said with a nervous giggle.

His knuckles brushed my hand. I held my breath, but he didn't notice the lavender tint creep across his knuckles…or he pretended not to. From the corner of my eye, I stole a look at him. *His eyes were as clear as blue glass, and although he was thin, his chest was solid and strong and—*

"Got to get going," he finally said, "but I'll be back."

"What makes you think I'll be here?"

"I'm not worried. Besides, I'm coming back with a rope."

"A rope?" I stiffened. "If you're even thinking of touching me—"

"What's with you, Purple Girl? Haven't you ever played *Snake*?"

"Can't say that I have," I said, regaining my composure. "How will I ever live with myself?" My lips hinted at a smile.

"Tomorrow, you won't be able to say that, Purple Girl," he said, getting to his feet. "I'll teach you what fun really means." He offered his hand to me.

I stared at his hand.

"Come on," he said, grabbing my hand, pulling me up. "I'm not afraid of a little purple."

My heart racing, I scooted to my basket, fished out two ripe tomatoes and tossed them to him.

"Don't you want them?" he asked.

"I've had enough tomatoes to last me a lifetime.

But little cakes dusted with sugar? I would do anything for those! I could eat them by the wagonload."

He smiled before disappearing over the stone wall.

And then it struck me; I didn't even know his name.

AND SO IT WENT ON. As soon as the golden-haired boy finished one of his odd jobs, he showed up in the garden. We made whistles from willow twigs and gave Waxy belly rubs and licked nectar from the few honeysuckles we could find. In the hours we spent alone, I got to know him, and one day soon rippled into another.

"We meet again," he said.

"I suppose we do. Sweeping ashes from a fireplace today?"

"What gave me away?"

I gestured to the soot on his cheek.

He shot me a smile. "Is your mother still in the village?"

"Busy hunting for work," I answered. "Papa is afraid the mill will close." Mama didn't suspect the daily habit of our meetings. *If she knew...*

"I have an idea, but you can't ask any questions."

"Can't promise."

"The less you know, the better. Just follow me," he said, making his way out of the garden. I bit my bottom lip.

He turned back toward me. "Trust me."

"Why should I trust you? You won't even tell me your name."

"Have some fun, Purple Girl."

"I don't think so."

"I know a way through the woods. No one will see you, and we'll be back before your mother returns to the cottage. What are you afraid of?" he asked, leading me out of the garden.

"If you only knew."

He unlatched the gate, and we set off, weaving our way through the forest before we cut through a field overrun with dandelions that ran behind Darby's farm. We circled the coachman's quarters by the big stone house and didn't stop until we reached the familiar shop at the bend of the road.

"The *bakery*?" I whispered, lifting a brow. My heart thumped against my ribcage.

"Would you expect anything less?" he answered, his lips curving into a lop-sided smile.

He crouched underneath an open window.

Breathless, I squatted beside him. “What are we doing here?” *Of all places!*

“Didn’t you say you would do anything for a little cake with sugar? Here’s your chance, Purple Girl.”

“But—”

“Aren’t you going to take it?”

I bit my bottom lip, this time to keep from smiling.

“I’ll climb through the window while you keep watch. Every Friday afternoon, when the baker is napping, his wife makes him sweet-meat. Once she pulls the goodies out of the oven, she sits in the rocking chair and waits for them to cool.” He nodded toward a side porch.

“Where is the baker’s daughter?”

“She’s out making deliveries.”

“How do you know all of this?”

“No questions, remember?” He put his index finger over my lips for a brief moment.

“You’re my look-out. Got it?”

“Sounds like the plan,” I said.

“I figure I have about ten minutes before the daughter gets back. If any of them find me in his kitchen, my goose is cooked.”

"And who said nothing exciting happens in Bilingham?" I asked, my lips quivering.

A side door slammed, and heavy footsteps clomped against the porch floor.

"It's time. Whistle if she goes back into the bakery. You can whistle, can't you, Purple Girl?"

"Hope I won't have to," I whispered. "Hurry!" With baited breath, I watched him climb through the window. Once I heard the soft sound of his feet hit the floor, I crept closer toward the side porch.

A piece of shadow came and went as a rocking chair creaked back and forth.

I suddenly heard the crunch of footsteps against the pebble-stone path and then the unmistakable voice of the baker's daughter.

She's early!

Chapter Seven

THE INVITATION

Instead of whistling, I moved closer to listen. I couldn't help myself.

"I have a proposition for you—" the girl started.

"Not another one," the baker's wife finished.

"I've run across the ringmaster of a traveling circus. He wants someone in his sideshow, and he will give just about *anything...*" she said, her voice trailing off, "for the girl."

"What girl?"

My stomach tightened.

"You know the one. Her blood runs purple. What if we snatch her?"

"You mean kidnap her—"

"Imagine the price we could fetch! The ring-master will take care of her—"

"Not a happy ending for—"

"The bearded lady, the dwarf, and the purple girl! All under the big top. I wonder what—"

A sudden crash came from inside the bakery.

"What was that?" The baker's wife rose from her rocker.

I whistled as loud as I could and scrambled toward the window just as my golden-haired boy tumbled through it and onto the grassy knoll. He had icing and sugar smeared across his bottom lip, and his pockets were full.

"Run!"

We took off like birds in flight. I was so quick my purple trail vanished with each new step. My heart pounded as I sprinted ahead.

A gunshot rang through the air.

When we finally reached the garden walls, we tore through the gate and collapsed in the grass. "Look." He opened up his hand to reveal little cubes made of chopped dates, lemon, hazelnuts, and sugar. "Turkish delight!"

"That's impossible! No one can get sugar any-more. It's too expensive—"

"It appears *they* can. Maybe they aren't who you think they are, Purple Girl."

"What happened in there? I heard a crash."

He held up his left hand. "I overlooked one minor detail—the pan," he said, blowing on his red and blistered fingertips. "*Hot*! Every crumb, worth every burn." He grinned and offered me the Turkish delight. "I hope I haven't discouraged you from a life of crime."

"Don't flatter yourself. I have a mind of my own." Flashing him a half-smile, I took a handful, but when I remembered the conversation between the girl and the baker's wife, I lost my appetite and refused all but a bite.

It was early in the morning when I found the boy nestled in the knotted branches of an old grandmother tree.

"Come up."

I tilted my head up toward the sky. "Don't think so."

"Why not? You can see everything from up here."

"Because girls don't climb trees."

"But they eat stolen Turkish delight?"

I shot him a look.

"Don't you want to try?"

"No," I lied.

"You're afraid, aren't you?"

"I'm not afraid of anything." My second fib.

"Grab a branch and pull up. It's easy."

"I don't feel like it." *The lies are coming so easily!*

"A girl who claims she's not afraid of anything is scared of heights? You never fail to surprise me," he laughed.

With my hands on my hips, I turned and stomped off toward the herb garden. "I'm not even afraid of a gypsy girl!"

He climbed down the tree to join me. "I bet you haven't even seen a gypsy girl."

Images of the gypsy girl darted across my mind. What did she know about my so-called golden key? I wanted to share these thoughts with him but did not. I couldn't tell him my secrets.

Not now. Instead, I handed him a slice of sourdough bread I had taken from the kitchen.

He kicked off his shoes and walked barefoot on the grass. "Meet me tonight," he said, pulling the doughy bread in half. "At midnight."

"Midnight?" My heart skipped a beat.

"Not a minute later," he answered, pushing a piece of bread into his frayed pocket.

I lifted a brow.

"For my baby sis, Beatrice," he said, patting his pocket.

I lowered my eyes. Although my parents were struggling, he was poor, and I knew it. There was a long silence before I met his gaze. "What's so special about midnight?" I asked.

"You'll have to come to find out. Slip out when your parents think you are sleeping."

"And why would I do that?"

"You'll see," he said, devouring the other half of the bread.

"I don't think so," I mumbled.

"I thought you weren't afraid of anything."

"I'm not, but—"

"But I'm tempting you?"

"Not at all," I said.

"Just give me half of an hour."

"I don't know—"

"I asked you to meet me at midnight, not get married."

"I can't promise—"

"I can," he said, grinning. "I'll be waiting."

AT MIDNIGHT…I slipped out of the cottage into the darkness.

Chapter Eight

ABANDONED

"I'm here," I whispered in the silence, my eyes adjusting to the black velvet of the night.

Something brushed my back, and I drew a breath, ready to let out a scream.

A hand clapped over my mouth. "It's me, Frankie," he whispered before letting go.

Frankie! My racing heart slowed.

"Here," he said. "Hold this." When he placed a sealed jar in my hand, I ran my fingertips along the tiny holes pierced in the lid.

"Follow me," Frankie whispered. He took my hand and by the light of the full moon led me toward the clearing in the back of the garden.

I stood stock-still. Hundreds of flickering lights buzzed by me.

"Lightening bugs," he told me. "The rarest lightening bugs in the world. They light up at midnight when the rest light up at dusk."

We stood there, in the night.

"Let's go," he said, twisting the lid off the jar.

Tripping over tree roots, giggling in the dark, I chased lightening bugs in the moonlight. When I caught one, I held the lid tight on the jar until I caught the next. I followed golden trails, bumped into Frankie, knocked into branches, and bit back laughter. A tree branch scratched my face, but I didn't mind. My jar, full of lightening bugs, flickered with lavender light...then glowed.

"Are you ready?" He stood so close to me I could feel his warm breath on my cheek. "One, two, three!" We pulled off the lids. Sparkling purple lights swirled around golden-white ones, streaking into the sky like shooting stars.

I stood in awe of the silent beauty whirling around us.

"Like a thousand sparks of..." I whispered.

"...magic," he finished.

We stood a moment longer, until the last firefly flickered and disappeared into the silky black sky. He took my hand. "Come on," he said, leading me

back to the cottage. His hand was warm, and my heart pounded as we stumbled our way through the garden, to the side door.

He leaned toward me, as if he might kiss me.

My heart was in my throat.

"Good night, Purple Girl," he whispered instead. And he was gone.

THE NEXT FEW DAYS in the garden were filled with Frankie's stories. I laughed until my sides hurt, howled until tears rolled down my cheeks, cried when he told me he was leaving for good.

"How can you leave me?" I blurted, my voice catching.

"My folks have to find work. We have family that can help us," he said, pointing to a spot on the horizon, "tucked in that mountain. An old, stone wall surrounds the village, one with seven gates."

"But there has to be some way you can stay!"

"Your family has a cottage. And you have this." He gestured to my garden. "Despite the drought, half of your garden survived."

"Don't you have a garden?"

Frankie shrugged. "You would be surprised."

"It takes a lot to surprise me."

"Let's just say my mother is happy when I scrounge up a potato from somebody *else's* garden."

"But—"

"I'll pick up more work...maybe run more errands. You don't know me like you think—"

"Can't your family manage a *little* longer?" I asked, fighting to keep my voice steady. "Just through the summer?" A heavy ache filled my chest.

He shook his head and turned his tired footsteps toward the stone wall.

"Frankie?"

He stopped and looked straight at me with his luminous blue eyes. "Purple Girl?"

My eyes blurred, and then an unexpected tear slid down my purple cheek. The weight of his impending departure felt—unbearable. My voice came out in a whisper. "You make me *laugh*, make me feel like I'm an ordinary girl."

"Trust me, you're anything *but* ordinary," he said, breaking into his usual smile. "You're more like a babe in the woods, so unsuspecting—"

"What does *that* mean?" I prompted, struggling to keep my composure. The garden would be barren without Frankie. I felt abandoned already.

"I heard you sing—from behind the garden wall."

I felt my mouth drop open.

"You're dangerous, Purple Girl." He threw his hand over his heart and lifted his chin to the sky. Off key he sung my words, mocking me lightly.

Soar through the skies
Free but precious...

"I don't sing like that but obviously you do!" I struggled to suppress an unexpected smile. Sniffling, I clenched my plum-colored fist at him in mocked fury, and for a moment, my mad laughter overtook my despair.

"I spied on you for days, Purple Girl, before we ever met," he said with a laugh. "Maybe I just wanted those vegetables from your garden. Maybe I'm not who you think I am—"

"You're rotten, Frankie!"

"Rotten to the core."

"I'm not going to miss you one bit," I hollered, half-laughing, half-crying, fighting to keep more tears from surfacing. I stepped toward him, so close to him. I wanted to kiss him, to feel his lips against mine.

The smile faded from his face as his piercing eyes locked with mine.

"Your voice is—beautiful," he said. "I'll come back, one day, Violet. I will," he promised. Then he took off and vanished over the stone wall.

Chapter Nine

DESPAIR

"Why so glum, Violet?" Mama asked. Dark circles shadowed her eyes. "You haven't been working in the garden."

I rolled my eyes. The hot, humid weeks following Frankie's departure were wretched.

Mama put down her rag and folded her arms. "We need every vegetable. Besides," she added in a gentle voice, "I miss your singing." She reached out and cupped my chin in her callused hands.

I jerked away from her.

She let out a sigh and pulled a burlap satchel off a peg.

A sudden thought rushed back to me. "Mama,

did you carry the bridal bouquet when you married Papa?"

She blinked in surprise. "Of course. Brides always do." With a faraway expression on her face, she handed me the satchel. "Princesses don't carry bouquets on their wedding day, though. They're the only ones. Now scoot outside, Violet."

I dragged myself to the garden, but the place felt bare and empty—*painful* without Frankie. I filled half the satchel with carrots and tomatoes before I wandered around the ancient oak at the far end of the garden. I froze.

Small slats of wood ran up the tree. Grips for my hands and holds for my feet!

"Oh, Frankie." I let out a sigh. I remembered waking up one morning to the hammering of a woodpecker. *It wasn't a woodpecker—it was Frankie!* I touched the holds and pushed down on them. They didn't give. The tree would be much easier to climb now.

I craned my neck and shaded my eyes and peered upward. As much as I wanted to climb that tree, the thought made my stomach flip. Maybe tomorrow. Maybe never.

I edged away, and as I headed to my favorite spot in the garden I gazed toward a large clearing in the garden. If I planted dogwood trees in the shape of a giant heart, would Frankie see it from the mountaintop? I dropped into the grass.

Papa appeared in the garden. "How dare you, Violet!" He held up the ancient book. "You swore you wouldn't touch it!"

I felt the blood drain from my face. "How did you find out?" I asked, getting back on my feet. "I was gentle. I didn't—"

"Three of the jewels were loose. You should have listened to me."

"I don't understand."

"A scholar younger than thirty doesn't have the wisdom or the knowledge to grasp it. He could misunderstand it."

"But why—" I started, breaking into a sob. I couldn't remember a time when Papa was angry with me.

"To the outside world, I don't have much, Violet, but as long as I have you, your mother, and *this book*, I have the world. And all of the answers!"

My heart sank. *Papa doesn't trust me.*

"Most children in your station aren't even taught to read." His deep voice sank to a whisper. "How selfish *are* you, Violet?"

His words stung.

He turned away and headed back to the cottage with his head down, shoulders stooped.

Flooded with hurt, I wiped the lavender dirt off of my hands and yanked a blanket off the clothesline.

The town-folks in Bilingham don't want me. Deep down Mama is embarrassed by me. And Papa keeps me hidden within the garden.

My heart tightened. *But Frankie dared to jump over the garden walls...*

My hurt suddenly turned to rage. Trying to silence the roar in my head, I spun away from the cottage and let out a single note. With the blanket in one hand and the satchel in the other, I unlatched the gate and walked out of the garden and into the road...alone!

Chapter Ten

ESCAPE

I would not lose the one friend I had in all the world. And I wanted *out* of the garden walls that imprisoned me. And if that precious book held all of the answers, my father should have ridded me of my purple long ago!

With Waxy beside me, I stuffed my blanket into the satchel and hurried forward, hugging the edge of the lane. Turning by the stables, we walked by the coachman's quarters and the stone house named Poplars. The stonecutter's wife appeared around the corner.

My hooded cloak! Why didn't I wear it? When the stonecutter's wife caught sight of me, she turned her head and scampered down the lane.

I let out a heavy sigh. Soon we passed the house with three stone chimneys, but instead of turning toward Bilingham's outdoor market, I fixed my eyes westward and set out on a secluded road headed toward Frankie's mountain. My heart pumping, I crossed Cherry Road. To my surprise, it was overgrown with blackberry bushes.

The sound of a horse and wagon yanked me out of my thoughts. I dodged a pothole before scooting down the grassy slope where I stood spine-straight behind a tree—careful not to touch it. I needed to be on my guard with strangers.

The wagon rumbled by.

Letting my breath out slowly, I wiped the sweat from my eyes and ventured out, traveling a few feet off the road amid the greens and browns of the forest.

After a while, we wandered farther off the road and into a grove of ancient trees where the air was cool and damp. With the tree trunks stretching hundreds of feet toward the sky, I was a dwarf walking among giants, stepping over their snake-like roots, searching for freshwater streams and berries before making my way back to the edge of the road. I hummed softly, my mind full of Frankie.

The day wore on, and one hour stretched into another. Night fell.

The wind moaned. Trees creaked. Dark shadows fell across the road. I stood by its side bewildered, straining to see the thick forest around me. I had never been alone in the night. Suddenly, Waxy took off.

"Waxy!" I whispered, struggling to see him in the shadows of the night. "Come back!"

He pattered through the woods.

"Waxy," I called, following his padded footsteps into the forest. "Come here, Boy." Fighting back tears, I threaded my way through the trees and into an open meadow.

He trotted back to me and then scampered farther ahead.

"Stop playing games, Waxy!" The moon hid behind the clouds, and it was even darker. Fear prickled through me and goose-bumps rose on my arms. "Where are you, Boy?" Grass swept my thighs as I made my way deeper into the black of the night.

Waxy stood before me. He nipped at my ankles and, before I could grab him, trotted farther into the field, where he disappeared once more.

"Where are you?" A gentle summer wind hummed and the grass swayed, brushing me as I groped my way through the dark. "Come back!"

Waxy darted back at me and romped around before he disappeared again.

"No more hide and seek, Waxy!" Black shadows hovered like ghosts. My mouth went dry, and cold sweat trickled down my back.

Soft paws pounced on my feet, and a wet nose nuzzled my ankles. I dropped to my knees and clung to my friend, feeling his face in the dark before I buried my face into his fur. "Oh, Waxy. Please don't leave me."

When I finally released him, I flopped into the grass and rolled to my back. Tucking my hands underneath my head, I looked up. Thousands of lonely stars dotted the black, velvet sky.

"Perfect place to sleep," I whispered.

Too exhausted to pull out my blanket, I stayed that way, late into the night, embraced by the skin of the meadow, nestled next to Waxy, in awe of the starlight above me. I didn't anticipate what was coming.

Something woke me. My eyes fluttered open. A star-studded sky floated over me. For a moment, I was dazed, unable to recall where I was.

A twig snapped.

Waxy lifted his head, then stiffened.

A pair of orange eyes glowed, locking with mine.

I bolted upright, my heart pounding. Waxy jumped to his paws and let out a growl.

The stranger in the meadow retreated, turning back toward the woods.

Waxy waited another moment, then dropped into the grass. His body remained stiff, his head cocked. Turning first to the left, then to the right, his wide eyes kept watch over me as the nighttime whispers of the meadow serenaded me into a restless sleep.

Chapter Eleven

A CRY IN THE NIGHT

I smelled Mama's sachet, the small cotton bag she kept filled with flower petals. Tucked between linens and bed sheets, the sweet aroma spilled out every time I pulled open the top drawer of her chest.

I jerked awake and struggled to remember where I was.

Waist-high flowers hovered over me.

I sat up with a start and then got to my feet. All around me, as far as my eyes could see, burst thousands of orange flowers. The meadow was brilliant and bright, blazing and wild, heavy with the scent of flowers. I glanced down at my feet, where purple, heart-shaped petals carpeted the forest floor. I knelt down. *Violets!*

Still dazed with awe, I plucked one and tucked it behind my ear.

"You led me here, didn't you, Waxy?" I nuzzled his furry wet face with my own, then reached for my burlap satchel. Fishing around for carrots and tomatoes, a flood of memories washed over me: my mother's picnics in the garden, the care she took braiding my lavender hair, the joy she took in charting my growth.

"You've grown another inch," she would beam, marking my height on the cottage wall before kissing my purple forehead.

I felt a lurch in my throat and swallowed hard.

"Come on, Boy." Waxy and I headed back, wading through the flowers out of the meadow and into the tree-studded forest by the road, the mountain still far out of reach. We walked onward, scanning for a natural spring and blackberry bushes or blueberry thickets. We plodded forward, a few feet off the road, passing creeping vines of wild cucumbers too bitter to eat, my head full of Frankie.

A dove cooed, and I answered back matching my voice to his. I could make my voice sound like anything. And then I spotted the village, surrounded by a pale-gray stone wall, tucked into the mountain. It rose in the distance.

A teenage boy suddenly emerged from the woods.

My pulse pounding, I crouched down behind an evergreen and anxiously waited for my purple footsteps to fade. *What will he do if he spots me?*

The boy stopped short as if he sensed me. Flashing a wicked grin, he spun on his heels and whipped out a knife. With the knife upright in his hand, he stood silent and still, posed to strike.

The blade—sharp for chopping! My gaze dropped to my plum-colored fingers. They would make perfect souvenirs to bring to his buddies…four fingers for four friends, a thumb for his best. Suddenly afraid, I curled them into a tight ball. *What if he—*

The boy slipped the knife back into his belt and ventured forward, disappearing down the lane. With a sigh of relief, I stepped out of the woods but into the path of a girl.

The girl looked right at me and stopped in her tracks.

Waxy chased after a butterfly.

I pushed past her, scurrying by, but somehow, she managed to get an arm around my neck.

"William!" she hollered from behind me, dragging me backwards.

"Let go of me!" I cried, pulling at her arm. "You're choking me!"

"She's purp-p-ple!"

The words clobbered me.

"Willia-a-am! Come back!" she hollered, tightening her grip on me. "You have to see this!"

I elbowed her in the ribs, once, twice, and a third time before I sank my teeth into her arm, and then, just like that, Waxy sprung at her.

She let out a startled scream, and I broke free.

Waxy and I took off! A hard rock pelted me on the side of my neck and then skipped along the road. The stabbing pain shocked me.

"Willia-a-a-m!" she wailed. "Catch her!"

With Waxy next to me, I ran down the lane. I clutched my satchel with one hand and reached up to touch my neck with the other. Everything was happening so fast. And then a second rock belted me, hitting the bony knob of my elbow, burning me like a bee sting. A third rock whizzed by me. *More footsteps behind me!* I glanced back over my shoulder…at the boy, at the girl.

"Look what the witch did to me!" she shrilled, pointing to her lavender-tinted hand and sleeve. "She used her black magic!"

As the boy stopped to examine her hand, Waxy darted deep into the woods ahead of me.

Blinking back tears, tangled in my skirt, I fled through the woods after him. I scooted down a slope and skirted around brier and dodged low branches until I was out of breath.

Choking back a sob, I crouched behind a hedge of twisted bramble and scrunched up tight. *Why can't I disappear?* I wanted to be a purple pebble amid the forest floor.

Waxy's padded footsteps trampled over the leaves as he made his way back to me.

A branch snapped.

I didn't move a muscle, didn't take a breath. *Why didn't I bring Mama's satchel, the one with her knife?*

My neck throbbed, and I bit my bottom lip to keep from crying as I strained to hear their voices, wondering if they were still hunting me. My aching feet, my grumbling stomach, the lump on my neck… it was suddenly too much for me.

I wanted, *wanted* to peel my purple off.

I put my hand under Waxy's belly and drew him closer. Still trying to catch my breath, I sniffled and rubbed the knot on my neck. My thoughts swam, and I wished myself back into the safety of my little garden. For the first time, I wondered if I should never have left home, and then I wondered if maybe, just maybe, it was time to turn back.

As if I had called on him, Frankie suddenly laced his way through my mind, and my thoughts soon turned to that night, at the end of our time together, when Frankie almost kissed me.

Frankie wasn't afraid of me.

I'm not a witch. I'm just me. I gently pressed my lavender fingertips on my neck. The welt still throbbed. Except for the buzz of hummingbirds and dragonflies and the breath of the woods, the forest was silent, the boy, the girl—gone. When my breathing finally steadied and the throbbing eased, I glanced at my purple hands.

I needed to disappear.

As a green garden snake slithered through the grass not far from us, the answer came to me. This will be easy, I told myself.

I was wrong.

The Purple Girl

When day folded into dusk, Waxy and I emerged from the woods. We passed a patchwork of vineyards and orchards and shadowy green fields. Clusters of cottages now crowded the hillside. Night fell like a black curtain.

Waxy led the way. As my eyes became accustomed to the darkness, I kept pace with him, my steps following his down the road and into the night, the path in front of us lit by the moon. I tried not to think about the dark…and what could be lurking in it.

Waxy plopped down and closed his eyes.

"Get up, Boy," I said, rubbing my tired eyes. "We slept all day." I could hardly make out the edge of the road in the faint moonlight. "We *have* to travel by night," I said, gently shaking him. My hairline was laced with sweat, and the welt on my neck ached. Something screeched in the forest.

Waxy whimpered.

"Hungry?" Fumbling in the dark, I reached into my satchel and poked around for food.

No tomatoes, no carrots—

Waxy let out a howl.

"Shhh." Stroking him behind his ears, I glanced over my shoulder. The dark spooked me. "Hush, sweet baby."

He howled again, this time louder.

My eyes begged the little guy to stop howling, but he was unstoppable. I was hungry, exhausted, and suddenly *homesick*. Panic rose in my chest, tears burned in the corners of my eyes, and I let out a little cry that turned itself upright and into a song.

Soar through the skies
Free but precious
I want to fly...

Waxy quieted. And then, over there, dimly lit by the moon and stretching over a small stream stood a wooden footbridge. My voice reached deep and weaved its way through the darkness as I headed toward the bridge. At the water's edge, I took a long swallow of water before I glanced back, praying Waxy would follow.

Up on all fours, Waxy moved forward. He dipped his head into the moonlit stream and lapped it up before he trotted behind me, catching up with my lavender steps. As we made our way across the footbridge, I belted out another note and held back a smile as the water rippled, then hammered to the quivering rhythm of my voice.

With each high note, the water rose. I held the note as long as could, and when I dropped it, the wave crashed, slapping the bridge. Cool water ran over my feet, tickling my ankles. I giggled at what I could do, then did it again.

With wet paws and feet, we plodded on, struggling to see in the night, grateful for the light of the midsummer moon. I hit a note so high, so clear, there was a rattle and then the crack of a nearby window shattering.

"Oh, no!" I gasped, my hand flying over my mouth. I had forgotten I could do that!

It suddenly struck me: How foolish of me—*to sing!* When my overture came to a sudden end, I heard a voice calling in the distance like a cry in the night.

"Who are you?"

Chapter Twelve

THE SEARCH

W*ho are you?* The words echoed.

I remained silent.

"Keep singing, please?" the voice called.

I hardly breathed, but my eyes caught a movement in a window.

"If you sing, I'll leave out a pot of rabbit stew for you."

My stomach rumbled.

"I'll light three candles and set them in the window, so you can find me."

Silence filled the air.

"My grandfather is confined to his bed," she said, her voice trembling. "Your song—helped him sleep." A golden trio of light suddenly illuminated the window. "Are you still out there?"

Waxy nudged me, and I took a deep breath before I called out to the stranger in the night.

"I'm headed toward the village, the one tucked into the mountain." My voice was unsteady. "It's surrounded by a stone wall."

"The Village of Seven Gates?"

My heart leaped. "Yes. I'm looking for a family that moved there. Their boy is Frankie. Do you know of them?"

"No." The answer came. "I'm sorry." After a pause, she added, "I'll leave fresh water by the stew. You'll sing, won't you?" The words echoed in the darkness, bouncing into each other. "Please sing. Your voice is like…an angel's."

A lullaby, my father's favorite, escaped from me as I made my way up the hill to the flickering light. I held each note as long as I could, trying to outdo the note before.

We reached the cottage.

Hidden in the shadows, I stopped singing and peeked toward the front door.

From a side window, flames danced on their wicks, casting flickering light on the doorstep. True to her word, the stranger had laid everything out. The stoop was cluttered with a footed tin cup, an oversized iron pot, a bowl, a dish, a spoon, and a jug stamped with three hearts to mark the number of gallons. My mouth watered.

"Come on, Boy," I whispered. With a side-glance, I crept toward the door where the aroma of potatoes and thyme and warm gravy greeted me. I scooped out a meaty portion for Waxy before I wolfed down the rest in big, hungry mouthfuls.

"To freedom and Frankie," I said, raising my cup into the air like I had seen my parents do once before when I spied on them from a half-closed door. For the first time, I wondered what they were toasting. After a long swallow of water, I wiped my mouth with the back of my hand.

With full bellies and hearts, we walked into the darkness, and I sang until dawn when both my feet and voice gave out. Wobbling like a circus clown, I slipped into the woods and behind a hedge where I curled up next to Waxy. The grass cushioned me, tickling my nose.

I was suddenly reminded of how, years before, I stumbled over a bucket of beige paint. I dipped my hands in the milky cream and spread it over my wrists and my cheeks and my neck, then smoothed it through my hair—so sure I wouldn't be purple anymore. At first, it tickled my nose, but soon clogged it. Caked in paint, my head spun. I could barely breathe. Soon I was gagging…gasping for air.

Mama was churning butter when she saw me swaying in the doorway. Her face went still before she exploded in a high-pitched scream. Mama was scared for me.

Putting my arms under my head, I closed my heavy eyelids and shut the memory away. As I drifted off into a dreamless sleep, my mind left Mama and wandered to Frankie, the gypsy girl, and then to the mysterious *Text of Wisdom.*

What secrets did it hold?

EXCEPT FOR a trio of flickering lights illuminating a window, the following night was dark, moonless. *Strange…three lights, again.* An owl hooted. A shadow moved across the pitted road. A shutter slammed, then latched for the night.

Waxy growled.

Something lurked in the forest. Still walking in the woods, alongside the road, I broke into a cold sweat. It was dark...and I was scared. The cottages I passed reassured me that people were nearby but also frightened me for the same reason.

A note escaped from my mouth, followed by another, and the singing calmed me, just as it had when I was in my garden back home. *Back home!*

I felt a pang of guilt.

I plodded ahead, pushing memories of home out of my head, replacing them with thoughts of Frankie. When my trembling finally eased, I quieted.

Flickering light interrupted the darkness. I gazed to the side and caught sight of a warm glow shining from a second-story window. Candles.

"Come on, Waxy," I urged, wondering about the candles.

A nearby window creaked opened.

I froze.

"Why aren't you singing?" A stranger's words echoed in the dark.

I dropped back into the shadows.

"Your voice is magic," the stranger called.

My eyes skated around the darkness.

As if he read my mind he said, "I'm over here."

I caught a glimpse of movement in a nearby window, a shape in the darkness. *So thirsty.*

"Please keep singing. My wife has fresh bread!" he called. "And she lit three candles, so you can find your way here." His words hung in the air. "I heard you were headed to the Village of Seven Gates."

I straightened in surprise. "You heard I was headed there?" As I asked the question, another trio of lights lit up in the distance, winking at me.

"You're close."

I drew a deep breath. "Is there talk of a new family in town? Their son is Frankie." I waited for a response before carrying on. "Frankie runs errands, picks up odd jobs—"

"No, I don't know of them. Where are you?"

I stepped back, farther into the shadows.

"Come closer. So we can see you."

I remained silent and still.

"Come into the light. And why aren't you singing? They told me if I left out food, you would sing. Warm bread..."

My stomach grumbled.

"Cold milk..." he lured.

Cold milk! Waxy danced on my feet.

With a half-grin, I gave in. I sang, my words pouring out like melted butter over parsnips as I plodded my way toward the light...and bread...and cold milk. The strangers here were bighearted, much more generous than the townspeople in Bilingham.

But they hadn't seen me.

ONE NIGHT ROLLED into another. We slept in the day, blazed lavender trails by night. I sang as I followed my way toward clusters of golden light, accepting generous gifts of bread and milk and honey, my head dancing with thoughts of Frankie.

Lost in my song, light in my step, my voice hit perfect pitch as I passed golden pools of light flickering in the windows. I wanted to hold Frankie's hand, wanted to get lost in his startling blue eyes, maybe even—

I came to a sudden stop. The Village of Seven Gates stood in front of me.

Chapter Thirteen

THE MAP

I stopped singing and craned my neck.

The pale-gray stone wall surrounding the village rose above my head, while row houses soared up the mountainside along tangled cobblestone roads. Waxy fell into step beside me, and side by side, we entered the village through an open gate. A random bolt of lightening split the night sky in half, flashing light on a three-legged dog as he hobbled along the road.

"It's you, isn't it?" A nearby voice reached me.

I stopped. Waxy stilled.

"We've been waiting. We heard about your singing. Heard that if we left candles in the windows, food by the door..." The girl's voice trailed off.

I strained my eyes to see her outline in the moonlight. "I'm looking for a family that is new to the village. They have a son, Frankie. Do you know them?" I said, wondering how many times I had asked this very thing.

"No." The answer came, echoing in the darkness.

"Do you know of a boy that runs errands—"

"No."

"and has golden hair—"

"No."

"—has a baby sister named Beatrice," I finished.

"Yes!" she cried.

My heart sprung open.

"On the other side of the village." Her words danced in the wind. "They're caretaking the House with Two Front Doors. I'm to your left, by the town's fountain. You can sleep in our barn."

I was too stunned to reply.

"You can have my bread pudding."

My heart pounded.

"I lit six candles. Six!"

When I didn't answer, she called out again. "Don't you want to sleep in our barn?"

If I slept there, she might stop by the barn in the morning and catch a peek of me in the early light. I couldn't risk it, but—

"It's empty. Only used for storing hay and wheat and barley."

"I've got to keep moving," I lied, hoping my wavering voice wouldn't betray me. I felt sticky with sweat. "But I'll take the pudding."

I gazed to my left and caught sight of a warm glow shining from a top window. And then I let out my song as Waxy and I set out, following our way toward the cluster of golden light. Once we passed the fountain, we reached her doorstep.

"Here, Waxy." I scooped out his portion of pudding before I scraped the bowl clean. As I let out a satisfying burp, a distant noise caught my attention. *Can't stay too long!*

I glanced over my shoulder.

Turned toward the moonlit fountain.

Looked to my left.

Looked to my right.

Rushed to the gurgling water.

As two stone lions stood guard on the walls, I leaned over the fountain's edge and splashed cool water on my sweaty face while Waxy paddled around in the purple-tinted water.

And then, by the silvery light of the summer moon, I caught sight of the nearby barn inviting us for a good night's sleep. "Come, on, Waxy." Certain the stranger didn't suspect anything, we followed the trail leading to the barn.

The door stood open, and the dirty sweet scent of hay and earth and timber spilled out.

I crept in, slid the heavy door closed, and dropped into my soft bed of hay. Waxy settled down beside me. *Hay.*

As I drifted off, a memory rushed to me. I couldn't have been more than four or five years old when Papa burst into my bedroom, wakening me in the night.

"Come on, sleepyhead," he said, ruffling my lavender hair. He waved me forward, then rushed to my mother and pulled her out of bed. Dazed, half-asleep, and still in our dressing gowns, we followed him outside toward a cart filled with hay.

"Get in!" he laughed, leading my mother by her elbow as I followed, rubbing the sleep from my eyes.

"What crazy thing are you up to?" Mama giggled, bewildered.

"You'll see," he said, waving his arms toward the cart in a grand gesture. He scooped me up and tossed me in next to my mother before Waxy jumped into the cart.

"Where did you get this thing? Who loaned it to you?" my mother asked, biting back laughter. Despite the dark, I caught the adoring look in her eyes when she gazed at him.

"It's time you two had an autumn hayride," he told us.

Waxy settled next to me.

Papa handed us warm cups of cider, then tucked a tattered blanket around us. A piece of hay poked out of Mama's mousy brown hair.

"We're off! Hang on, Violet," he laughed. My mother and I exchanged sleepy, bemused looks. We didn't own a horse!

With his back to the cart, Papa grabbed the wagon arms and shouted, "Ne-e-e-eigh!"

Mama and I hooted as he pulled the cart forward, scraping down the lane and around the bend toward Bilingham's outdoor market.

The villagers slept in their little nests…while Mama and I snuggled in the back with Waxy, giggling and sipping on our cider amid the hay…unseen. For the first time, I was invisible.

And I wasn't afraid.

I never loved Papa more than at that moment. I had never felt so free.

THE FOLLOWING MORNING, the sun wove its fingers through the barn's open window. A pigeon in the rafters fluttered, a faraway rooster crowed. My eyes landed on a yellowed slip of paper jutting out from underneath the barn door.

I rushed over and unfolded it. Hand-drawn lines, symbols, and there, toward the top corner of the map and circled in red: the House with Two Front Doors. Apparently, the stranger guessed I would show up.

I folded the lavender tinted map and tucked it into my satchel before I peeked out the barn door. Did I risk traveling in the morning light? If I didn't, I risked the stranger returning to the barn, finding me here…*seeing* me…

I drew a deep breath and crept out of the barn. Waxy and I traveled along vacant side streets, meandering our way around the sleepy town until we stood in front of the House with Two Front Doors.

I wasn't prepared for what awaited me.

Chapter Fourteen

FRANKIE AGAIN

I was surprised. The house rested on a tended lawn and was larger than my cottage back home. It had a sprawling front porch and oversized windows flanked by freshly painted shutters. A door stood at each end next to large urns of blush-colored roses. Twins. I glimpsed at one door, then the other. I did not know which door to knock on.

From somewhere behind the house, I heard the murmur of voices, then the sound of laughter. Waxy's ears pricked back.

I smoothed my hair, attempting to tidy it, and tried to forget that my blouse was ringed with sweat, my skirt with stains. I glanced at Waxy. With his nose now to the ground, he shifted his attention from a grasshopper to a mound of marching ants.

More laughter pealed.

My breath quickened as I turned and wandered around to the back of the big house where I froze in my purple tracks. There he stood, smiling that sweet smile of his, clad in clean clothes that fit his sturdy body.

My heart leaped. Frankie was just as handsome as I remembered! But he had changed. No longer thin, no longer drawn. No more soot on his cheeks. Even his eyes shined brighter. I wanted to say something—but all I could do was stare.

Who is the girl on the swing?

Her pale hands clutched the ropes as she gazed up at Frankie with eyes that were large and dark and wild.

I peered at Frankie in dizzy disbelief as he leaned to the pink-cheeked girl and whispered in her ear, saying something I couldn't make out. "Oh, Frankie," she teased, letting out a high, nervous giggle.

I stared at him, mystified. *This is not happening.*

Frankie suddenly looked up, as if he sensed my presence.

I took one step toward him but slipped behind a hedge before he caught sight of me. Straining to hear them, I peeked at Frankie between prickly stems as his gaze wandered back to the girl.

He leaned toward her as if he were about to kiss her. Instead, he playfully tugged a strand of her hair. The girl puckered her rose-colored lips, then cocked her head to the side and grinned, her easy smile showing off teeth that were square and white.

I thought I was going to be sick. With horrified eyes, I stared at them, terrified of what was coming.

The dark-eyed creature slid off the swing and placed her palms against Frankie's broad shoulders as if to steady herself. In a fluttery voice, she murmured something before she stood up on the balls of her feet, stretched her neck toward him, and pressed her lips against his.

I lost my footing and tumbled into a bush.

Frankie pulled away from the girl and turned toward me. "Violet?"

My cheeks burned. I scrambled to my feet. With Waxy behind me, I spun on my heels and sprinted back through the twisted streets.

"Violet!" he called after me.

I raced by the fountain, down the trail, and

into the barn. *Ple-e-ease don't come in here!* Short of breath, I peered between the wooden slats and watched Frankie rush past the barn before he disappeared into the maze of cobblestone streets.

I stumbled to one of the back stalls where I threw myself into the hay and wept into the early night...my teardrops turning the straw purple.

BELLS AWAKENED ME. Footsteps echoed. I peered outside as villagers gathered by the fountain, lanterns swinging.

Something was about to happen.

I grabbed my satchel and led Waxy out the door. My eyes adjusted to the dark as we edged our way toward the fountain and hid deep in the shadows, away from the crowd.

The magistrate stood on a platform facing them. "Two carrier pigeons arrived," the bald little man bellowed.

The crowd stirred with excitement.

The odd little man cleared his throat. "The first carried a strange message from the queen's men." The magistrate lifted a bushy brow before he puffed on:

"'We are looking for Violet. You will know her upon seeing her.'"

I felt my face flush and took a step back, dropping my head to the ground.

The magistrate shrugged, perplexed, then wiped his brow with a handkerchief. "Does anyone know this Violet?"

My heart hammered.

"Speak now!" he demanded, stomping his undersized foot.

The villagers chatted among each other.

A queasy feeling simmered in my belly as Waxy and I edged away from the crowd.

"The second message…" He stopped and waited for the commotion to die down.

"The second message," he repeated, "is an alert. It simply reads:

"'Thieves from other villages looted the towns of Coventry and Bilingham. Not only are the bandits stealing food and money, but they also are searching for a jeweled book, one mentioned in an ancient legend. Riots have taken to the streets, villagers are homeless, cottages have been—'"

Bilingham! I fled down the dark cobblestone streets toward the base of the mountain.

Bilingham! I had to get home.

In my panic, I tripped over my own two feet and landed on my hands. The scrapes burned. Bruised and breathless, I picked myself up but got tangled in my skirt. My hands felt sticky with blood, and my lower lip was split. My timing could not have been worse.

"I know who you are—"

I tried to move past the stranger, but she grabbed my arm.

"Violet!"

Waxy growled.

"You're Samuel's daughter, from Bilingham, aren't you?"

I froze and struggled to recognize her face in the dark; the sharp bird-like features, the large gap between her two front teeth. "Who are you?"

"I was your mother's midwife." Her fingers dug into my arm as she told me about the wicked night I was born. "You were a curse from the start," she finished. "The terrible shock of you turned your father's black hair *white*."

Waxy bared his teeth and tucked his tail.

"Only the devil's child—"

"I'm not the devil's child! I'm not a witch—"

"I should have buried you in the forest when I had the chance!"

I pushed her away from me and broke free.

A villager appeared from around the corner.

"The circus master will pay good money for her!" the midwife hollered, pointing to me.

I ran for it.

"Wants her to be the star of the freak show!" she screamed.

Sprinting down the alleyway with Waxy at my heels, I quieted myself in the habit I knew. I let out a ballad, hitting one high note and then another, raising the pitch of my voice higher and higher until my racing heart settled. And as I did, a cluster of lights flickered from one window, then another. The town, and soon the countryside, was showered with twinkling lights. Golden light shined—lining the roads leading me to home.

Chapter Fifteen

CAUGHT

As I sang under a starlit sky, horses thundered down the road. The ground shook as one horse rushed to my side, a second stopped in front of me, and three more clopped from behind.

I stood rock-still in the black of the night. Waxy stiffened as his ears pricked back.

The man on the first horse swung his lantern. "We know it's you, *Violet*."

A shudder skipped down my spine. In the overlapping shadows of the night, I couldn't read his expression.

"We've been looking for you. On every village corner, every doorstep—they talk about you," said the messenger, his baritone voice deepening. "The constant chatter, the rumors…stories of you spread like a wildfire. The queen wants to hear you sing—for herself."

"The queen?" My throat tightened.

"The queen is also ready for her son to take a wife." He gestured to me.

"Me?" I squeaked.

"You."

Waxy growled.

My mind spun. Is that why the gypsy girl wanted my voice? Did she know it would attract the attention of the queen?

His horse whinnied. "Your voice could be very—" He stopped himself.

"My voice could be *what*?"

"Your singing would be useful to the prince, especially when he becomes king."

"*Useful!*"

"It's not every day a commoner can marry royalty. Although the queen wonders if you really are…"

I swallowed hard before I spoke. "Most girls would marry a prince—"

"—without hesitation," he finished.

But I would only marry for love…even if it

meant...never at all. I was suddenly scared and didn't know what to do.

"The queen, the prince—they always get what they want," he said.

Drawing a deep breath, I stepped into the lantern's light. With trembling hands, I pulled back a handful of tangled strands and pointed to my purple face.

The messenger's mouth dropped open. He swung the lantern closer to me, his eyes raking over my face. "The story...it's true," he said, suddenly pulling out his sword. "I didn't believe it." He lifted my chin with its cold, sharp tip, then tickled my throat with it.

Don't move a muscle, don't take a breath. One jab of his blade and—

"Don't touch her!" cried one of the soldiers.

"She'll cast a spell on us!" cried another.

"But the queen ordered..."

The messenger withdrew his sword and waved the others forward before they vanished into the night.

I let out a deep breath. We were set free. The soldiers were more afraid of my thirteen-year-old self than the queen!

Chapter Sixteen

UPWARD BOUND

It was early in the morning, and Waxy and I stood outside Bilingham. Trees swayed, a child wailed in the distance, and a burnt stench surfed on the edge of the wind. We plodded forward, over the scorched earth, down the country lane.

I slowed down by the house with three stone chimneys. It was dark and shuttered. My chest tightened, and we picked up our pace and walked on, passing the stone house named Poplars. Broken windows, shattered glass, blood on the cobblestones!

Waxy and I took off, crisscrossing our way through yards, darting up the lane, and racing across the pasture until I reached home. I stumbled to a stop, dazed.

The proud garden walls stood, but our cottage had turned to ashes. The fireplace and a few blistered walls remained, and the chimney still reached for the sky, but the staircase led—to nowhere.

I could see Mama and Papa trapped within walls of fire, screaming amid the flames. Maybe Mama's dress caught fire, maybe her.... I pushed the terrifying images away, but other pictures of Mama came into my mind. I pictured Mama lighting the fire on the stove and lacing up my boots. I felt her gentle kiss upon my forehead.

And Papa? His sturdy arms, his smile, his voice...*gone*? Burying my head in my hands, I cried softly. Hot tears streamed down my cheeks. The thoughts haunted me. The grief strangled me—I could hardly breathe.

Trying to steady myself, I leaned against a tree and mopped my eyes. The brown bark rippled into plum, my purple trickling through the branches to the highest leaf. Waxy lifted his head to me and licked my purple hands while I tried to catch my breath.

I wiped my nose with my sleeve, and then, as my eyes roamed the wreckage, I spotted something poking out of a mound of ashes. *Mama's rabbit figurine!*

As I picked him out of the rubble, something jingled. I wiped the roasted rabbit with my skirt and kissed him before I tucked him in my satchel. And then, peering into Waxy's amber eyes, I buried my face into his sweet and dirty smelling fur.

Something in my mind suddenly clicked, and the hair on my arms stood straight.

I bolted toward the mound of rubble and dug through ashes until my fingers grazed the velvet book-cover. As I pulled out the *Text of Wisdom*, the little bells chimed.

Kneeling in the dirt, I wiped off the ash. The jewels beamed with purple light as I removed the cover and opened the book. I thumbed through the pages.

Gypsies:

1. *An ancient nomadic people dating back to the 14th century. Keepers of a unique wisdom; known for casting spells and using palmistry, crystal balls, and cards for fortune telling.*

2. *Numerous legends of Gypsies kidnapping children.*

In the margin a scribbled note read:

> *Do gypsies have magical powers? Yes, but ONLY if the mortal BELIEVES they do.*

I tried to digest the words, but thoughts of my parents floated back to me, and my eyes clouded with tears. A lavender tear rolled down my purple cheek and onto the page. The words blurred, colors swirled, and like a reflection in a pond, a scene on the page rippled before it emerged.

Sound rose from the page, the book heated in my hands, and somehow the words wriggled and stretched and formed themselves into a moving picture, like a one-act-play unfolding before my very eyes.

> *Two monks perched on a bench like blackbirds. "No one suspects he's growing up here, Brother John. He's safe, hidden in the monastery."*
>
> *"Three years since we rescued him."*
>
> *"He loves playing in the woods, but he can't venture far. People aren't ready for him."*
>
> *"And as soon as he tries to talk—"*

"They will accuse him of being the devil's child or—"

"I'll explain it to him once more," said Brother John, lifting his eyes. "Here he comes." A crinkled smile flashed across the monk's face as a little boy jumped into his arms.

The boy's orange-speckled eyes locked with mine, then they widened with surprise. He opened his mouth to speak, but instead of words, waves crashed, trees rustled, lightening cracked, brooks gurgled, winds whistled, and a thousand other earthy sounds rolled out of his mouth at once. He quickly pinched his lips shut, and there was silence.

My heart stopped. The orange-eyed boy had nature's voice!

The boy turned to the monk and used his hands to make a sign and a quick gesture, and then with two fingers, he pointed to his eyes...and then to me.

As their heads turned, the images on the page swirled like wet watercolors, the pictures faded into muddy colored puddles…and, just like that, the monks and the boy were gone.

The page was blank.

A thought jolted me. There are *two* of us in this world. The boy is not the devil's child! He's not magical. He's simply…himself.

As I started to close the text, something caught my eye. The inside back cover bore a note in Papa's loopy handwriting. It read:

> *Blessing or curse? That is what Violet must decide. It's Violet's destiny, and she has the power to change it.*

I sat in silence for a long time. Finally, I dressed the book and tucked it into my satchel.

Suddenly, noise rose in the distance, and a boom rang through the wind. There was the sound of glass breaking, gunshots, and dogs barking. When a baby wailed, my sadness suddenly turned to rage. With the satchel over my arm and Waxy by my side, I took off.

And then I let loose—in the daylight! I released a note and raised the tone of my voice higher and higher, my voice straining with grief, trilling like I never had before.

Churning out my painful song, I moved onward with Waxy by my side. We followed the rutted lane as it snaked by dandelion yards and cottages. We passed an overturned cart, then Widow Collin's cottage and Wakefield Place and Dragonfly Hill.

A villager emerged in her doorway, while another peered at me from a window. As the stonecutter's wife rounded the corner, she turned her head to me, and for the first time, her eyes searched my purple face.

I marched ahead. Piping out another refrain, I reached the outdoor market, where the yard swelled with people. Some held pitchforks while others carried clubs. One by one, their heads turned toward me.

And through it all, I couldn't stop my furious singing.

The crowd jeered, a woman screamed, an old man wept. Someone lit a torch.

I raised the pitch of my voice, hitting a note so high it hung on a silver thread. The arguing thinned to scattered voices, and the crowd hushed.

Then I pushed it even further. I delivered a high sweet note that bounced off my tongue like sugar, the words tickling my lips. Feet shuffled behind me.

And I sang louder. I couldn't help myself.

By the time I reached the last twist in the road, I felt the crowd gathering behind me. Quickening the tempo, I pushed out a high weightless note and crossed the overgrown lawn by the cathedral.

My voice rose as my eyes landed on the granite statue. Still trapped in weathered stone, the larger-than-life angel beckoned me forward. Her fingernails were now painted green! When I met the carved out hollows of her eyes, I knew where I was headed.

The bell-tower loomed over me.

With a crowd following in my purple footsteps, I approached the oversized doors and tugged the iron handle.

The door didn't budge.

Still singing, I yanked on the handle again.

"It's locked! You can't go in the bell-tower."

In mid-note, I turned to face the town magistrate.

"It's you." The silver-haired man stepped back, his small eyes widening. "I should have known." A ring of keys dangled from his overstuffed pocket.

I surprised us both by bursting out another note, and while my violet eyes lingered on his astonished brown ones, I yanked the keys out of his pocket and turned away from him. With a slight tremble in my hand, I slid the largest key into the lock and turned it clockwise. I heard a quiet click before the heavy door creaked open.

The door sprang wide, revealing rough limestone walls and a handful of open-air windows. I led Waxy inside and looked up. A circular staircase spiraled around the tower, winding its way to the top, and the ceiling soared above me, making the tree in the back of my garden suddenly seem small.

Waxy settled on the uneven stone.

It's time.

I placed my satchel by Waxy's side. As Waxy pressed a paw over it, I tucked up my long skirt into my waistband and pointed my feet in the direction of the staircase. Taking a deep breath, releasing another note, I headed toward the stairway. The white stones faded into violet underneath my footsteps.

I looked up. The stairs went on and on, narrowing toward the top. Drawing a deep breath, I hit one high-pitched note, then another. The notes echoed through the bell-tower, pranced along my purple steps, and bounced around me. My voice swelled, filling every hollow space.

I felt a little dizzy, a little short of breath, but I edged my way upward, spiraling around and around the bell-tower. As one hand moved along the banister, the other swept the wall for better balance, the rough stone cold to the touch. Although the tower's staircase had various landings for resting, I chose—perhaps foolishly—to keep going.

The steps narrowed. My heart pounded. My fingertips brushed the wall. I climbed higher and higher, breathing hard, singing harder, inching my way up toward the top.

What compelled me to glance down? I'll never know. But when I did, I was astounded.

My purple strokes decorated the walls with a thousand shades of violet twisting and fading and colliding like a turning kaleidoscope. It was a living, breathing *masterpiece*!

And without shame, in response to all of the fear that stemmed from the horrible day of my birth, I released another note.

Suddenly, my ankle wobbled, my knees shook—and the tower spun around me.

I clutched the railing. I stopped moving, stopped singing, stopped breathing. Frozen to the spot, I didn't dare look down. If I tumbled to the bottom, I would hit the white stone floor like a drop of purple paint. I tried not to think about it, but of course I thought of little else.

When the spinning rocked to a standstill, I swallowed hard and looked up; I was so close to the top! Turning back was not an option.

Breathe. Breathe. Sing my way to the top. I steadied my knees. *Sing. Sing. One step at a time.* I steadied my breathing.

I regained my focus and my footing and my singing voice—and climbed higher and higher one step at a time, until the staircase abruptly ended in front of a trap door.

I pushed open the door and climbed through, and like a bird perched high in her nest, I found myself on an open rooftop enclosed by a balustrade. The giant bells hung behind me.

And there I stood, on the rooftop, my feet slightly apart, my spine aligned, my abdomen flat… singing at the top of the bell-tower.

Almost free!

When I looked out, I was shocked into a momentary silence.

Hundreds of townsmen had flocked below me. They weren't grabbing for the same head of lettuce, and they weren't blaming anyone for their bad luck. No elbowing, no jabbing, no overturned carts. Instead, the townspeople stood mute and still, craning their necks and shading their eyes to catch sight of me.

I felt the golden light shine upon my purple face, and with my face pointed toward the sun, my violet hair blew softly in the wind. I resumed my singing as an unexpected image of the gypsy girl darted across my mind—she was right! I *have* my golden key.

My mind skipped back to the answer hidden in the *Text of Wisdom*, the words I had stumbled across so many days ago:

> *A mystical key that unlocks one's very soul. Each golden key is uniquely cut to fit a specific mortal.*

I released a high note and then another and held it long and steady. Soon strangers were clasping hands, peering at me in all of my purple.

The note pierced the air.

I wasn't afraid.

Finally, I unlocked it. I released my final note; so high and sharp and clear, it danced along the wind, cut through the valley, and sliced its way across the meadows.

I pushed the note as far as it would go, letting it float on without end, free, until even its echo softly faded to nothing. The note had been cut free, and I was left empty, gasping for breath. My voice was my golden key that unlocked everything for me. Breathless, I grabbed hold of the stone banister and closed my eyes.

The mob below me remained silent.

When the sound of horses galloping reached my ears, I opened my lavender eyes. *What had I done?*

Chapter Seventeen

THE PURPLE GIRL

The crowd parted to let the horseman through. Dressed in a gray uniform, the messenger cupped his hands around his mouth, so I could hear him. "Good day," he called, in the deep voice that I immediately recognized.

I remained motionless, peering down from the top of the bell-tower.

Still on horseback, he bowed to me.

My mouth dropped open. He bowed…to *me*?

"I carry another message from the queen," he hollered, his words echoing in the unnatural silence. "The queen still wants to hear you sing—for herself."

I remained silent. My purple handprints marked the balustrade, but no one seemed to notice—or mind.

"You shared your voice, letting it ring through the countryside, over the hills—at great personal risk."

Unlike me, he didn't seem so frightening in the light.

"The queen wants to bestow you with a gift." His chocolate brown horse twitched, shifting his weight from one leg to the other.

"Me?" I squeaked.

He patted the horse's neck. "She asked me to bring her wizard." A frail man with long, ginger-colored hair and a bird-like beak of a nose snaked to the front of the crowd; he was a man I hadn't noticed until now. Without a saddle, bridle, or reins, the wizard's horse trailed a few inches behind him, moving like his shadow.

The wizard and then the horse stepped forward.

The messenger straightened, then cleared his throat. "The gift," he said, nodding toward the wizard.

I shrugged, confused.

"The wizard can drain *all* the purple from your skin."

I felt my mouth drop open.

"You will look like everyone else."

I gaped with gratitude.

He smiled with dimpled cheeks, his words still floating in the air.

Fighting back unexpected tears, I gripped the balustrade. My eyes darted from the baker to the baker's daughter to the butcher and then to a group of children. My hands trembled.

"Do you accept the queen's offer?"

The air was filled with waiting. I gazed at the people below me, dizzy with knowing.

The wizard, then the horse, moved closer.

I now understood what I was destined to do but wondered if I had the strength.

"Can you hear me?" he hollered.

I summoned my courage.

"Do you accept the queen's offer?"

My mouth quivered, then I cleared my throat. "I am happy to sing for the queen, but I can not accept the gift."

The crowd gasped.

"You're refusing the gift?" He stared at me openmouthed.

I tried to still my shaking hands.

"There must be something she can give you?"

A pause.

"Insulting the monarchy—"

"The town needs repairing," I said. "The school, the rutted roads, the bells in this tower." I gestured to the bells behind me. "And if the monarchy could spare more seeds for the farms, I would be grateful. We will rebuild our own cottages, but your start—"

Then I spotted them in the crowd. My eyes locked with my mother's, then landed on my father. A sudden wave of calm washed over me.

Papa smiled. He gestured to me, to my mother, and then brought both hands to his heart. "I have everything," he mouthed to me. Mama grabbed him and kissed him on the lips.

"Consider it done, my lady," said the messenger, tipping his hat.

I bit back a grin. No one had ever referred to me as a *lady*!

As the messenger turned to leave, he paused, then guided his horse back in my direction. Craning his neck, he shaded his eyes and called out to me once more.

"Don't you want to be rid of your purple?"

I smiled. "No."

Epilogue

TODAY

After the incident in the bell-tower, the baker never charged my family for flour. To this very day, decades later, the baker's wife loads my arms with fresh breads and insists that I taste her cakes, free of charge.

The butcher welcomes me into his shop and only sells my family the finest cuts of meat.

The town flourishes, crops thrive, bells peal. Most of the villagers shake my hand. Some still thank me. And when the children see me, they reach out to touch me. They giggle when the tips of their fingers brush mine.

Frankie kept his promise. Years later, he returned—bearing a wagonload of little sugar cakes.

If it weren't for his luminous blue eyes, the steadiness of his voice, and his wide grin, I would have struggled to recognize the brawny man that stood before me. I met his wife, a lovely woman, and their five boisterous children. Biting into the cakes, Frankie and I laughed as we reminisced about the few, but precious, weeks we shared in the garden. And when I told them about the time I refused to marry royalty, Frankie flashed me a knowing grin. He knew me all too well.

After the incident in the bell-tower, I returned the *Text of Wisdom* to my father. In unspoken consent, neither Papa nor I ever referred to it again. Yet, on my thirtieth birthday, I found a plain unmarked box mysteriously left by my door. The ancient text was inside, and a note was tucked underneath it. I recognized the loopy handwriting. It read:

Protect it.

Because a woman is forbidden to study the *Text of Wisdom*, I will not confess to studying it late at night while my family sleeps…or to midnight meetings where a small group of women gather around me. And when my not-so-royal husband lifts a brow at my suspicious behavior, I hold back a grin. How much trouble could I get into—a woman like me?

I will admit to one secret…the gypsy's prediction came true. I did *not* throw a bridal bouquet at my wedding. Instead, I honored the centuries-old tradition in my husband's family. I carried a sprig of golden wheat to ensure a bountiful harvest and a fruitful life.

And do I sing? Of course! My children's offbeat, but angelic, voices often join mine. We are our own symphony.

And as I listen to them sing, I gaze at them. Although they have my high cheekbones, my deep-set eyes, even my curls, they don't have one drop of my purple…but I love them anyway.

For Discussion

1. In what ways is Violet less-than-perfect?
2. Although Violet experiences discrimination, does she discriminate against any one in the story? If so, where?
3. Does Waxy realize that Violet is purple and looks different from everyone else? If so, does he care?
4. Violet's story occurs long ago. If the story took place today, how would it be different?
5. What time period do you think Violet's story takes place? What clues does the author give you? Why doesn't the author provide a date?
6. Why do you think the author chose the color purple? If you were the author, what color would you have chosen for the main character and why?
7. Why wasn't Violet destined to marry Frankie?
8. What fears did Violet conquer by the end of the tale?

9. Why aren't Violet's children purple? Did they gain or lose something by not inheriting her color?
10. Is this story more about social acceptance or self-acceptance? Family or friendship?
11. Violet left a purple trail wherever she went. In what ways do people leave their marks?
12. Violet grew up behind walls, separated from others. Who could she represent?
13. Does Violet's dangerous, night-time journey and escape remind you of any other persecuted groups?
14. Did the story end the way you expected? Could there have been an alternate ending?
15. Does the author reveal why Violet was purple? If not, why?
16. Pretend you are the author. If you wrote a sequel about one of the minor characters, who would you write about? Why?

About the Author

As a writer, and also a designer of tapestries with a Bachelor of Fine Arts degree from the University of Georgia, it is only natural for Audrey to weave visual stories. When she is not designing tapestries, she is busy conjuring up characters that find themselves in extraordinary

situations. Between carpools and design work, she is plotting, scheming, writing, and revising. She lives in North Carolina with her husband, their three children, and her unruly dog, Rascals. Audrey's favorite time to write is in the early morning while her family sleeps. With Rascals sprawled out snoring beside her, it only takes one oversized cup of coffee to get her mind moving.

Audrey is a member of the Society of Children's Book Writers & Illustrators. She loves traveling, museums, and blackberry-apple pie. Actually, she loves all kinds of pie. And she especially loves her family. They have put up with Violet and Waxy for a long time. You can visit her at: www.audreykane.com.

About the Illustrators

Tory and Norman Taber have been working as illustrators for over twenty years. Together, they have developed a style that

accentuates their collaborative process. Playing off each other's strengths, they create illustrations for children and young adults. In addition, both teach in the Art Department at Plattsburgh State University. They live in the small town of West Chazy in the foothills of the Adirondack Mountains, with their two not-so-purple girls, Zoe and Elizabeth. You can see more of their work at www.toryandnormantaber.com and www.wendylynn.com.